BILL COSBY

LITTLE BILL BOOKS FOR BEGINNING READERS

My Big Lie

by Bill Cosby

Illustrated by Varnette P. Honeywood

Introduction by Alvin F. Poussaint, M.D.

SCHOLASTIC INC.

Cartwheel B·O·O·K·S®

New York Toronto London Auckland Sydney

Assistants to art production: Rick Schwab, Nick Naclerio

Library of Congress Cataloging-in-Publication Data

Cosby, Bill, 1937-
    My big lie / Bill Cosby; illustrated by Varnette P. Honeywood.
      p.   cm.— (Little Bill books for beginning readers)
    "Cartwheel books."
    Summary: Little Bill gets in big trouble when he tells a fib to explain why he has come home late for dinner.
        ISBN 0-590-52160-8 (hardcover) 0-590-52161-6 (pbk.)
    I. Honeywood, Varnette P., ill. II. Title. III. Series. IV. Series: Cosby, Bill, 1937- Little Bill books for beginning readers.
PZ7.C8185 Bi 1999
[Fic]—dc21
                                                       98-42049
                                                      CIP
                                                      AC

10 9 8 7 6 5 4 3 2 1   9/9 0/0 01 02 03 04

Printed in the U.S.A.   23
First printing, May 1999

To Ennis,
"Hello, friend,"
B.C.

To the Cosby Family,
Ennis's perseverance against the odds
is an inspiration to us all,
V.P.H.

Dear Parent:

Little Bill's parents have a problem. Their son has come home several hours late, missing his dinner and worrying his family. Even worse, he has lied about where he went and what made him late, telling a whopper about getting into a van with a man who stopped to ask him for directions. His parents can't believe he would be stupid enough to get in a van with a stranger. It's only when his father says he's going to call the police that Little Bill blurts out the truth: "Nothing happened. I made it all up."

His parents are too mad to praise him for admitting his mistake, but they don't yell at him. Instead, they send him to his room to think about his actions—and to copy an old folk tale, *The Boy Who Cried Wolf.*

It's a story that shows why it is wrong, even dangerous, to lie, and Little Bill is impressed. But he's also worried. The townspeople in the story no longer trusted the boy who falsely cried "wolf." Will his parents be able to trust him after this? Once again, his parents act thoughtfully. They understand that although their son disappointed them today, one bad choice does not make him a bad *boy*, and to Little Bill's relief, they tell him they do trust him.

Because his parents gave him a punishment that was educational, Little Bill was able to learn that lying is a serious mistake. Because they didn't yell at him when he finally told the truth, he will be less likely to lie the next time he gets into trouble. And, because they expressed their confidence in him as a person, Little Bill, like most children, will try harder in the future to live up to his parents' expectations.

Alvin F. Poussaint, M.D.
Clinical Professor of Psychiatry,
Harvard Medical School and
Judge Baker Children's Center,
Boston, MA

MOREHOUSE
B
The Boy Who
Cried Wolf
Once upon a
time there
was a

Chapter One

Hello, friend! I'm Little Bill. Sorry. I can't play with you now. I have to stay in my room and think about what I did wrong. To help me think, I have to copy a story called *The Boy Who Cried Wolf*.

It's about a boy who takes care of sheep, which seems like a boring thing to do. What can he do for fun? He can play a tune on his pipe. He can talk to his dog. He can talk to his sheep. BORING!

One day the boy wants to stir up some excitement. So he yells out, "WOLF! WOLF!"

All the people from the town stop what they are doing. They grab their hoes and their rolling pins and their axes and they run to help the boy, because wolves like to eat sheep.

The boy thinks it's pretty funny to see all the grown-ups with their axes and hoes and rolling pins. And he laughs. The grown-ups go away— and they are MAD!

Well, two days later, this boy is bored again. He's already played all the tunes he knows on his pipe. He's already said all he has to say to his dog. And he's already said all he has to say to the sheep.

So what does he do? You guessed it.

He yells out, "WOLF! WOLF!" And all the people from the whole town stop what they are doing, grab their hoes and rolling pins and axes and run to help the boy. And the boy laughs and laughs and laughs. The grown-ups go away even MADDER than they were before!

Then, one evening while the sun is setting and the shadows are creeping, a wolf with huge fangs and drool pouring out of its mouth jumps out of the bushes. The boy cries, "WOLF! WOLF!" but the grown-ups don't come. They think the boy wants to laugh at them. They think there is no wolf.

But there is. And he eats up all the sheep—every last one. It was an ugly scene.

Now can you guess why I'm being punished? I cannot tell a lie. I told a fib—a BIG FIB.

Chapter Two

I was rushing out the door when Dad stopped me. "And where do you think you're going?" he asked.

"I'm going to ride my bike out to the pool," I said. "David Chow said he was going out there to practice for the swim meet. I told him I might practice with him."

"You don't have time," said Mom. "We're having an early dinner. We're eating at 4:30."

"I'll be back by then," I said as I ran out the door.

I was riding past the basketball courts when I saw a whole lot of the guys.

"Little Bill," Andrew called. "Get off that bike and come here fast. We need you on our team!"

Oh, man! I wanted to go play. Andrew, Fuchsia, Kiku, and Michael were playing with some other kids.

This is what I thought I'd do. I'd play basketball for just a little bit and help Andrew, Fuchsia, Kiku, and Michael out. Then I'd go meet David Chow. And then I'd go right back home.

Chapter Three

We won! We played good defense.
We rebounded well. We passed well.
We got good shots. We played a
great game and we won!

I was too excited to go home by myself. I walked my bike so I could go home with Andrew and Fuchsia. We laughed and talked about how great we were. But as we got closer to my house, I remembered what my mother had said.

"Does anyone have a watch?"
I asked.

"Nope," said Fuchsia.

"I do," said Andrew. "It's seven o'clock."

"Seven o' clock! How did it get to be seven o'clock? I'm in trouble," I said. "I should have been home at four-thirty."

"You're in BIG trouble!" said Andrew.
"You'd better think of something fast."
Then Andrew and Fuchsia crossed the
street to go to their homes. I was just
half a block from mine and thinking
fast!

Chapter Four

Turning the doorknob, I was dragged inside by the force of the door being pulled open. Mom, Dad, Bobby, and my great-grandma, Alice the Great, crowded together in the hall.

This was worse than I expected. And I expected it to be bad.

My father's voice boomed above the rest. "Where have you been?"

"Are you in trouble!" Bobby said.

"Give the boy a chance to talk," my mother said.

"Yes, give him a chance," Alice the Great repeated.

Mom started talking again. "When you were late, we went to the pool to look for you. No one saw you there all day. David Chow said you never showed up. We were so worried."

"Give the boy a chance to talk," said Dad.

"Yes, give the boy a chance," said Alice the Great.

There was a sudden silence. I could even hear Dad's watch tick. I could even hear the goldfish move pebbles in the tank. I could even hear my heart beat.

"I was riding my bike to the pool."

"Yes," said Dad.

"I was riding past the basketball courts…"

"Yes," said Mom.

"…when a man in a car called, 'Hey, kid.' So I went over to the car."

"How *could* you!" Bobby said.

"He asked me how to get to Harry's Ice Cream Shop. So I told him. But he didn't understand my directions. So I told him that I would show him, and I got in the car."

"How *could* you!" said Bobby.

"What did you do with your bicycle?" Dad asked.

"It was a van. He put it in the van. I sat in the front seat and gave him directions, but he made a left turn when I told him to make a right turn. And I started to worry that I shouldn't be in this car, uh van, with this stranger. So when he stopped at a red light, I quickly opened the door and ran home."

"What about your bike?" said Mom.

"Oh, I ran to the basketball courts, where I left my bike and raced home."

"How *could* you!" Bobby said.

"What color did you say this van is?" said Dad.

"Green."

"And what make?" Dad asked. He walked to the phone.

"Uh, I don't know," I said. "Who are you calling?"

"Officer Nuzzi," said Dad.

"But nothing happened. I'm okay," I said.

"Something could have happened, Little Bill," Mom said. "Officer Nuzzi will want to know about this."

I had to tell the truth. I didn't want to repeat my big lie to Officer Nuzzi.

"NOTHING HAPPENED," I said. "I made it all up."

"We knew you were lying," Bobby said. "First you told us you put your bike in the van; then you told us you left it at the basketball courts!"

You can imagine what happened next. Dad was mad, Mom was mad, Alice the Great was mad. And Bobby was glad that he wasn't in my shoes.

Chapter Five

You know what? Mom, Dad, and Alice the Great were right to be mad at me. I made a big mistake. Lying is a bad idea.

I was copying *The Boy Who Cried Wolf* when Mom and Dad walked into my room. I was glad to see them. I was very worried about something.

"In the story, the grown-ups stop trusting the boy. They don't come when he needs them. And the wolf eats his sheep," I said.

"That's right," said Mom.

"That's right," said Dad.

"Will you ever start trusting me again?" I asked.

Mom and Dad looked at each other, then looked back at me.

"I trust you," said Mom.

"I trust you," said Dad.

Then they gave me a double hug. I'm a very lucky boy. And that's the truth!

HOWARD L. BINGHAM

HOWARD L. BINGHAM

Bill Cosby is one of America's best-loved storytellers, known for his work as a comedian, actor, and producer. His books for adults include *Fatherhood*, *Time Flies*, *Love and Marriage*, and *Childhood*. Mr. Cosby holds a doctoral degree in education from the University of Massachusetts.

Varnette P. Honeywood, a graduate of Spelman College and the University of Southern California, is a Los Angeles-based fine artist. Her work is included in many collections throughout the United States and Africa and has appeared on adult trade book jackets and in other books in the Little Bill series.